SHOUTYKID is a great book... if you like Diary of a Wimpy Kid or Tom Gates you will like this book... it's really funny and it made me laugh.

Isaac, age 8

Amazing and funny, I loved it! Harry Riddles is a great character... He does silly things but is pretty smart.

Frank, age 8

D0557400

Probably the funniest thing I have ever read.
Tom, age 9

Amazingly funny.
Rohan, age 8

Shoutykid is one of my favourite books... it is awesome!
Harley, age 9

Unlike any book I've ever read.
I loved it!
Sam, age 10

Anyone who has read it
can't not love!
James, age 10

Awesome, epic, funny and
entertaining.
William, age 9

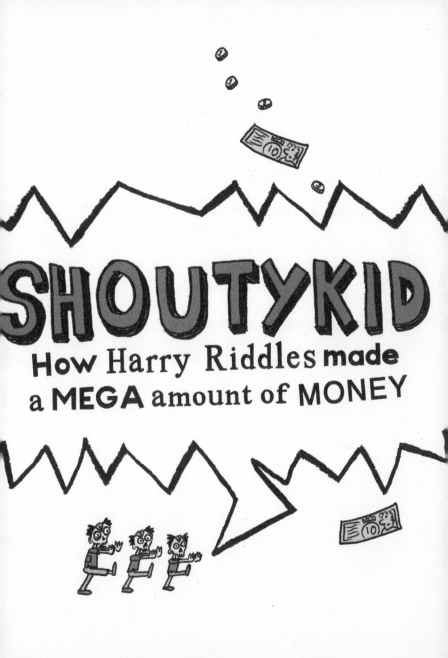

By the same author:

Shoutykid – *How Harry Riddles Made A Mega-Amazing Zombie Movie*

Shoutykid – *How Harry Riddles Mega-Massively Broke The School*

Shoutykid – *How Harry Riddles Got Totally Nearly Almost Famous*

Shoutykid – *How Harry Riddles Totally Went Wild*

SHOUTYKID

How Harry Riddles made a **MEGA** amount of **MONEY**

by SiMon MaYLe

Illustrated by Nikalas Catlow

HarperCollins *Children's Books*

First published in Great Britain by
HarperCollins *Children's Books* in 2017
HarperCollins *Children's Books* is a division of HarperCollins*Publishers* Ltd,
HarperCollins Publishers
1 London Bridge Street
London SE1 9GF

The HarperCollins website address is:
www.harpercollins.co.uk
1

ISBN 978–0–00–815892–7

Printed and bound in England by Clays Ltd, St Ives plc

MIX
**Paper from
responsible sources**
FSC www.fsc.org **FSC C007454**

This book is for Gem xxx

From Harry Riddles **to** Charley Riddles
Subject: School trips and other stuff
26 March 20:04 GMT

Dear Cuz –

School starts next week and TBH, I can't wait. We have a class trip up to London. Have you been? Mr Forbes is taking us to see a musical, ride the Underground, go on a big red sightseeing bus, plus do some other cool stuff. And the best part is:

we won't be going with Charlotte or mum, so NO
SHOPPING. YAY!

What's going on in California?

GBTM soon.

Yr cousin,

Harry

From Charley **to** Harry
Subject: School trips
26 March 12:07 PST

Cuz –

I'm teaching lacrosse to kids, which is cool,

but my dad's on my case, so I'll probably head back to college this w/e and start training.

From Harry **to** Charley
Subject: Training
26 March 20:09 GMT

Training? Yeah? Me too (hopefully).

From Charley **to** Harry
Subject: Training
26 March 12:10 PST

You too what?

From Harry **to** Charley
Subject: Training
26 March 20:12 GMT

Gonna start some training.

From Charley **to** Harry
Subject: Training
26 March 12:13 PST

For what? You don't play sports.

From Harry **to** Charley
Subject: Training
26 March 20:15 GMT

I play eSports. And the new WoZ game drops in

like three weeks,
so I've got plenty
of training coming
my way.

From Charley **to** Harry
Subject: eSports
26 March 12:17 PST

No offence, H. But sitting on your rear eating
Doritos and blasting zombies is not what most
people call training. You know what I mean?

From Harry **to** Charley

Subject: eSports

26 March 20:18 GMT

Yeah, but that's because most people won't have PLAYED this game, cos this game is NEW – but when they do, they'll discover that you can't sit around eating Doritos, cos the game is called World of Zombies RUN! And you play it on your phone. That means you have to RUN! Or, you get EATEN! You should definitely get it. It's gonna be awesome!

From Charley **to** Harry
Subject: WoZ Run!
26 March 12:25 PST

I don't think so.

From Harry **to** Charley
Subject: WoZ Run!
26 March 20:30 GMT

You're not gonna download it?

From Charley **to** Harry
Subject: WoZ Run!
26 March 12:31 PST

Nope.

From Harry **to** Charley
Subject: WoZ Run!
26 March 20:33 GMT

Why not?

From Charley **to** Harry
Subject: WoZ Run!
26 March 12:35 PST

When you grow up a little, you'll see you won't want to game all the time. It's what happens.

From Harry **to** Charley
Subject:WoZ Run!
26 March 20:37 GMT

Yeah well maybe for
you, but not me.
I haven't grown for
like a year.

From Charley **to** Harry
Subject: Growing up
26 March 12:39 PST

That must suck.

From Harry **to** Charley
Subject: Growing up
26 March 20:41 GMT

It does if you have a sister called Charlotte. She said if I don't start growing soon, my life will be hell when I go to big school in September, cos I'll be the smallest kid there and they'll pick on me. I said if that happens, I'm not leaving Mount Joseph's.

From Charley **to** Harry
Subject: Growing up
26 March 12:49 PST

Everybody has to move school, H. Even YOU.

Yeah, well if it was up to me, I'd probably never leave, cos my school is GREAT!

From Harry **to** Dad
Subject: The Razor Death Adder Chroma Mouse
10 April 18.04 GMT

Dear Pups,

Before you FINALLY come home (which is gonna be WHEN exactly?), plz don't forget what we talked about last night on Skype. Just in case you have forgotten, what we talked about was the incredible and totally amazing Razor Death Adder Chroma Mouse. This is the best gaming mouse EVER made and if you bring me home one of these suckers, I PROMISE I will mow the lawn every weekend, and not get into any more fights with my stupid sister — even when she tries telling me I'm so small I should be living under the floorboards like one of those kids in *The Borrowers*.

From Dad **to** Harry
Subject: A Death Mouse
10 April 19:07 CEST

My kid,

I didn't say I'd bring you back a Death Adder as
a homecoming present. I said I'd get you that
mouse for your birthday. So even if I buy it, you
can't have it until July, cos it's a birthday present,
not a business trip present. But the way things are
going, I don't think I'll be home until June anyway,
so you'll have to wait a little longer, OK? But do
me a favour – do not wind up your sister! Your
mother has enough on her plate without you two
fighting all the time.

Pups x

From Harry **to** Dad
Subject: Charlotte
10 April 18:09 GMT

I won't wind her up as long as she doesn't wind me up. But the only way that's gonna happen is if I GAG her. (And BTW, I don't think Mum would be too mad if I did).

From Dad **to** Harry
Subject: School
10 April 19:11 CEST

So how's school? Good to be back?

From Harry **to** Dad
Subject: School
10 April 18:12 GMT

No.

From Dad **to** Harry
Subject: School
10 April 19.14 CEST

Why not?

From Harry **to** Dad
Subject: School
10 April 18:18 GMT

Cos all the after school Special Activity stuff has been cut. So now we have no dodgeball. No school of rock. No ultimate Frisbee. Everything has just STOPPED and there's nothing for me to do when I have to wait for Charlotte to finish hockey practice. Mr Phelps said that's what happens when your school runs out of money. What does that mean?

From Dad **to** Harry
Subject: School
10 April 19:25 CEST

Mum hasn't talked to you?

From Harry **to** Dad
Subject: School
10 April 18:26 GMT

No.

From Dad **to** Harry
Subject: School
10 April 19:27 CEST

Mr Forbes told us the school is having some money problems. That's why there's no dodgeball after school. But they hope to sort everything out soon and then everything will be fine. In the meantime, why don't you spend some of your free time writing to your grandma and tell her how much you're looking forward to staying with her this summer?

From Harry **to** Dad
Subject: School
10 April 18:50 GMT

Maybe. I gotta go now. *The Simpsons* are on TV.
Night, Dad xxxx

From Harry **to** Dad
Subject: School
11 April 17:20 GMT

Pups,

I don't think everything *is* going to be fine. Mr
Forbes wasn't in school today, cos he fell off his
bicycle. Ed Bigstock said that's what happens if
you're the headmaster and your school owes like a
MILLION POUNDS. You have a heart attack and fall
off your bicycle.

From Dad **to** Harry
Subject: School
12 April 09.12 CEST

Is Mr Forbes going to be OK?

From Harry **to** Dad
Subject: Mr Forbes
13 April 18:27 GMT

Mr Grigson told us that Mr Forbes will be back in school soon, and that we shouldn't worry about our school trip, But who cares about the school trip if the school is like a million pounds in debt and everybody is gonna lose their job?

From Dad **to** Harry
Subject: Mr Forbes
13 April 19:29 CEST

Your school is not a million pounds in debt!

From Harry **to** Dad
Subject: School
13 April 18:31 GMT

Is it more?

From Dad **to** Harry
Subject: School
13 April 19:32 CEST

No!

From Harry **to** Dad
Subject: School
13 April 18:34 GMT

Then maybe I'm gonna be OK.

From Dad **to** Harry
Subject: School
13 April 19:34 CEST

Why? What have you done now?

From Harry **to** Dad
Subject: School
13 April 18.37 GMT

Jessica told Bigstock that I could raise that money
and save our school.

From Dad **to** Harry
Subject: School
13 April 19:40 CEST

Why did she say that?

From Harry **to** Dad
Subject: School
13 April 18:43 GMT

Cos Bigstock was being an idiot teasing this kid in Year 3 and saying that he was never going to finish school, cos when Mount Joseph's closes, that'll be it. The kid will have to find a job in a sweatshop.

When the kid heard that he got pretty upset, cos he's only seven. And that's when Jessica told him

not to worry, the school will NOT be closing and
Bigstock goes, "Yeah? Who's gonna stop it?" And
you know who Jessica points at? Me.

From Dad **to** Harry
Subject: School
13 April 19:51 CEST

Well, we should have a family meeting and see what we can come up with. Maybe your mum could bake some cakes?

From Harry **to** Dad
Subject: School
13 April 18:54 GMT

How many cakes are we talking about?

From Dad **to** Harry
Subject: School
13 April 19:57 CEST

Well, the shortfall is about £7,000, so that's – I don't know, 2,000 cakes? Maybe a little less.

From Harry **to** Dad
Subject: Cakes
13 April 19:00 GMT

That's a lot of baking. Even for Mum.

From Dad **to** Harry
Subject: Cakes
13 April 20:03 CEST

Then maybe you need to get busy and start writing.

From Harry **to** Dad
Subject: Cakes
13 April 19.05 GMT

That's what I thought.

CHAPTER THREE
THE ZILLIONAIRES

From Harry **to** Elon Musk (ElonMuskOffice@
TeslaMotors.com)
Subject: My School
14 April 20:21 GMT

Dear Elon Musk, multi-zillionaire owner of Tesla,
SpaceEx and SolarCity, hi there!

My dad read your biography and he said
basically you're the sort of guy I should work for
when (and if) I ever get any bigger. He said not
only do you have some really cool companies,
but also you LOVE TO GAME!!! Is it true that
every Friday night at your office at the SpaceEx
rocket factory in Los Angeles, you play Quake
against the guys who work for you? He says you
also like BioShock and Warcraft, but he didn't
know if you played World of Zombies – which is
my number one game.

Anyway, like you, I really love rockets. Me and my dad have made a few. We built this one called the Alpha Maxxi and after three good launches my dad decided we needed to take it to the next level and MAN OUR SPACECRAFT. So Dad volunteered Brian. Brian is a snail who lived in my dad's vegetable patch. Dad hated him, cos Brian was always eating his lettuces. So Dad finally got his revenge by Sellotaping him to the outside of our Alpha Maxxi capsule. Luckily that worked out OK for Brian, cos I packed the parachute, so when the engine flamed out at 750 feet, the parachute popped, and that snail returned safely to our field. Now I've retired Brian from astronaut duty and he lives in a box up in my room. I feed him Dad's lettuces or – on special astronaut treat days – some of Mum's carrots.

Anyway, here's the thing. My headmaster is a really nice guy. He's called Mr Forbes, but he was in hospital, cos our school might close and it's been stressing him out. I have to go to big school in September, but if I can I want to help save

Mount Joseph's, cos if it closes, then Mr Forbes and lots of other nice people like him are going to lose their jobs. Plus, Jessica told Bigstock that I could definitely do something. That's why I'm writing to you.

Please can you send Mr Forbes a cheque for £7,000? In return I will get Ed Bigstock to sign up for your Mission to Mars. This kid's a real doughnut and if I told him I could guarantee him he'd get at least a hundred new followers for his Instagram account, he'd probably jump into one of your rockets TOMORROW. Plus, his dad is a polar explorer, so his family loves going to places that are cold and nobody else wants to visit. The only problem is this trip might make his head swell up even bigger than usual. But I figure if it will save our school, it's probably worth it.

Plz GBTM soon, then I can tell Mr Forbes that our school will stay OPEN!

Good luck and have fun. (And BTW, my dad says your cars are really cool)

Harry
harryriddles1@gmail.com

From Harry **to** Mrs Steve Jobs, (laurene.jobs@
superschool.org)
Subject: My Super School
17 April 20:22 GMT

Dear Mrs Steve Jobs, wife of the genius inventor of
the iPhone, the iMac and all that other really cool
computery iStuff, hi there!

As a mum, I'll bet you're just like my mum – really
nice. Do you like stray cats? My mum does. If she
sees a stray running around in our back garden,
she'll be out of the back door with a can of cat
food faster than you can yell, "Here, Kitty!"

Anyway, after dinner last night we were talking
about school stuff and Mum told me that you've
started this thing called The Super School Project,
which is a competition to come up with a school

that suits today's modern needs. She said you're prepared to give the five winning schools ten million dollars EACH in prize money.

Well, that's about nine million, nine hundred and ninety thousand dollars more than we need to keep my school open. But let's say we entered your competition – this is what I would do to make our school even more SUPER.

First, I've been telling Mr Forbes every lunchtime
that we need a room dedicated to gamers like me
– which is what we had when I had a computer
club. But this hacker kid called Guy Fox ruined
it for us when he hacked our school computer
network and pranked the local police and
firemen, which BTW got me in lots of trouble.
So that would be my first suggestion: get our
gaming room back.

Next, I'd buy a decent hearing aid for Mr Morrison.
Mr Morrison is one of our best teachers. He says
he's older than Moses, but I think he's probably
lying. He teaches us religious education, but he's
almost deaf now, so he mumbles A LOT. If you give
him a new hearing aid that works, maybe we'll
all start getting As instead of Cs, cos then we'll be
able to hear what he says.

Finally, I'd install a rocket launch pad in our playground. That way we could send Ed Bigstock up to Mars. Do all these things and I believe we would have a SUPER school (and one with no more bullies – yay!!!).

Plz send the winning cheque to Mr Forbes at Mount Joseph's School.

That's all I have to say.

Good luck and have fun.

Harry
harryriddles1@gmail.com

CHAPTER FOUR
CLASS MEETING

World of ZOMBIES
COMMUNITY FORUM

19 April 17.32 GMT

 Kid Zombie: Walnut - u online?

 Goofykinggrommet: Hey, Harry - wussup?

 Kid Zombie: Not much.

 Goofykinggrommet: What's going on at yr school? My dad said it might have to close.

Kid Zombie: Maybe.

 Goofykinggrommet: U writing to anybody about it?

 Kid Zombie: Everybody.

 Goofykinggrommet: Like?

 Kid Zombie: The Prime Minister, Richard Branson, Elon Musk – lots and lots of people.

 Goofykinggrommet: Any luck?

 Kid Zombie: Not yet.

Goofykinggrommet: Lol.

 Kid Zombie: I know.

 Goofykinggrommet: So what r u gonna do?

 Kid Zombie: My teacher wants us to talk about it in a class meeting and see if we can think of something.

 Goofykinggrommet: You know what I'd do? A sponsored surf paddle. U know - like paddle from Black Rock down to Cambeak?

 Kid Zombie: I was thinking we should pull an all-night gaming mega-marathon!!!

Goofykinggrommet: OMG, that would be like so cool!

 Kid Zombie: You think?

 Goofykinggrommet: You gonna ask?

 Kid Zombie: Everybody would just laugh at me.

 Goofykinggrommet: Did I tell you we're moving?

 Kid Zombie: Where?

 Goofykinggrommet: Australia.

Kid Zombie: AUSTRALIA!!!

 Goofykinggrommet: Yeah.

 Kid Zombie: WHY?

 Goofykinggrommet: Dad says we'll have a better life.

 Kid Zombie: Than Cornwall?

 Goofykinggrommet: Yeah,

 Kid Zombie: You want to go?

Goofykinggrommet: Bigger waves. Always sunny. Maybe.

 Kid Zombie: That totally sucks, Walnut.

 Goofykinggrommet: We can still play World of Zombies!!!

 Kid Zombie: It won't be the same!!!

 Goofykinggrommet: I'm really sorry, Harry.

Pups, Walnut's MOVING!!!
Harry

Where?
Dad

AUSTRALIA!!!

When?

Soon, maybe!

U OK about that?

NO! He's my best friend! I don't want him to go! He's like the only person I ever hang out with at the weekends!

Well maybe we can all go out and visit. That would be fun, right?

When?

I don't know. Soon.

This summer?

This summer we're going to Spain.

So when then?

Let's talk about it when I get home.

If you lived here, we could talk about it now.

From Harry **to** Charley
Subject: Class meeting
21 April 19:23 GMT

Cuz –

Today we had a class meeting to see if we had
the next Lord Sir Alan Sugar in our year. You know
what? We don't. The only good idea I heard
in thirty minutes of yakking was Bulmer's. He
wanted to charge people to go worm-charming.
Have you tried it? Basically you get twenty
minutes to charm as many worms as you can.
The person who charms the most worms, wins a
prize. Each person pays five pounds to enter. So
if every parent in the school pays to play, then
that's 5 x 120, or £600 – which is a pretty good
haul, right?

Bigstock liked this idea a lot, too, but that's probably cos he said if we did it, he'd win (obviously). And he'd win cos he'd bring his guitar and play 'em Motörhead. He says worms LOVE loud noise, and it doesn't get

louder, or noisier than Motörhead. What do you think?

GBTM soon,

Yr Cuz,

Harry

From Charley **to** Harry
Subject: Class meeting
22 April 12:24 MTZ

I don't know about Motörhead. I'd give those worms some Metallica.

From Harry **to** Charley
Subject: Class meeting
23 April 19:36 GMT

Well, we're not giving 'em either, cos basically
Miss Bradshawe told Bulmer that worms were
pretty yucky and we should think of something
else. Jessica said we could do pony rides on old
Thunderbolt and charge a pound. But any idiot
stupid enough to climb on the back of that bad-
tempered old horse would be taking their lives in
their hands, cos he always BOLTS.

Anyway, then Bigstock told Miss Bradshawe
that his dad wants to SPONSOR our class on a
FUN RUN. So he's going to pay us one pound
for every mile we run on the Camel Trail. When
Miss Bradshawe heard the kerrchinggg!!! of

Mr Bigstock's generous offer, she said, "What a brilliant idea, Ed! Let's start with that!" So that's what we're doing: A fun run from Wadebridge to Padstow. But I've done the maths and even if 25 of us kids complete the course, we'll only make 25 x 6 which is £150. Bigstock said that's still £150 more than anything I could come up with. And you know what? He's right. I've written to tons of celebrities and multi-zillionaires, but nobody is writing back and nobody wants to help. Now I don't even know if I should bother any more.

Squid,

Don't quit just cos they aren't writing back.
Keep plugging away and you'll get a break.
QUITTING IS FOR LOSERS!

BTW, the idea behind a sponsored run is you
get LOTS of sponsors, not just Bigstock's
dad.

CHAPTER FIVE
BLESSING IN
DISGUISE

Pups, Mum said you're not coming back this w/e, cos they need you to work for another three weeks, but you should come home earlier cos basically Mum and Charlotte are AT WAR.
Harry

What do you mean?
Dad

Charlotte's a kleptomaniac and can't stop stealing Mum's clothes. Plus Charlotte lies a lot. She even tried telling Mum that she's probably got something wrong with her brain, cos she forgot that she gave Charlotte some belt when she went off to Walnut's parents' goodbye party. Mum said if she had given Charlotte the belt, she would have remembered, but she doesn't remember, because she didn't give it.

Your poor mum.

We need you here, Dad. But in a perfect world — let's just imagine that Charlotte wanted to move out, you wouldn't stop her, would you?

When did Charlotte say she wanted to move out?

Yesterday. It was the first piece of good news I've heard since Bigstock got foot-and-mouth disease back in January.

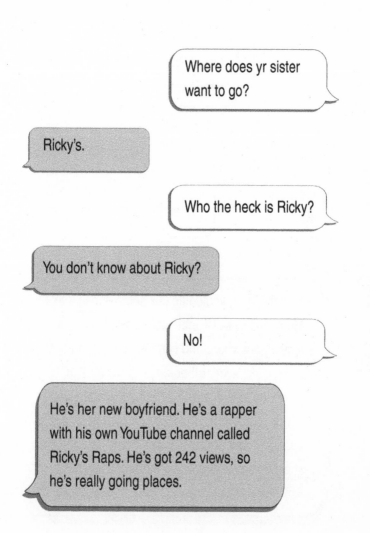

Where does yr sister want to go?

Ricky's.

Who the heck is Ricky?

You don't know about Ricky?

No!

He's her new boyfriend. He's a rapper with his own YouTube channel called Ricky's Raps. He's got 242 views, so he's really going places.

I liked Spencer! What's wrong with old LD?

GONE!

I need to come home!

Exactly! Then you could talk some sense into Mum, cos basically she said Charlotte's not moving anywhere and can take the bus into college like every other kid in Cornwall. But Charlotte said she'll never get the grades she needs to become a human rights lawyer if she's spending four hours on a bus every day, cos she'll be so exhausted by the bus ride. That's why she needs some digs in Truro with Ricky.

She sounds more and more like your mother. I'm gonna call her!

Why? If Charlotte moves out, it's win/win for us. No arguing with you, and no wedgies for me! It'll be GREAT! BTW, can Ricky come over and graffiti your skate ramps? He says he wants his next video to look like he's in the South Bronx – wherever that is.

It's in New York City where there's lots of graffiti. We live in North Cornwall where there's lots of cows and no graffiti.

So that's a no?

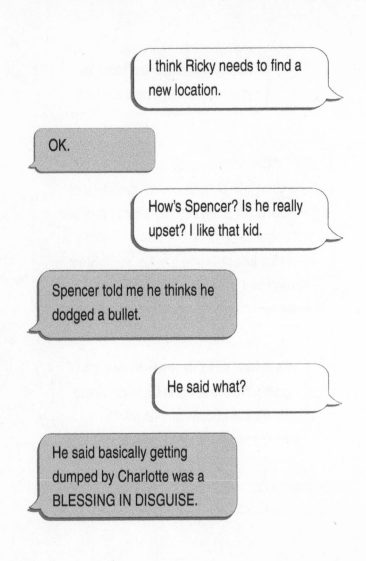

I think Ricky needs to find a new location.

OK.

How's Spencer? Is he really upset? I like that kid.

Spencer told me he thinks he dodged a bullet.

He said what?

He said basically getting dumped by Charlotte was a BLESSING IN DISGUISE.

That's not nice. If I see Spencer again, I'm gonna talk to him!

Well, he's not going anywhere.

What do you mean?

He came by the house last night to pick up his Xbox controller and Mum told him just cos him and Charlotte weren't going out, didn't mean that he should be a stranger and disappear from our lives. I just hope he doesn't decide our house is now a cool place to hang out, or I'm going to have to hide all the chorizo cos that kid empties the fridge every time he comes.

CHAPTER SIX
THE FASTEST SNAIL
ON EARTH

HIS ROYAL HARRYNESS

Tresinkum Farm
Cornwall PL36 0BH
25th April

Lord Alan Sugar
Amsprop Estates Head Office
Amshold House
Goldings Hill
Loughton
Essex IG10 2RW
UK

Dear Lord Sir Alan Sugar, moneymaking genius
and global TV personality, hi there!

My teacher is one of your greatest fans and
said if we had a ten-year-old version of you in

our class, we'd have a real chance of saving my school from closing. She said a kid like you would probably have a million and one brilliant moneymaking ideas, which could easily earn my school the £7,000 we need to stay open.

Well, I have a pretty cool idea for a new business. It's to do with my snail. He's called Brian. He lives up in my room in a cardboard box and was trained as an astronaut, but is now retired. Recently, I have begun to realise that Brian may have another amazing career ahead of him. Actually, it wasn't all my idea. Spencer (he's my sister's old boyfriend) was in on it, too. Basically, what happened was, it was dinner time for Brian in my house, so I got him some lettuce from the fridge and when I came back I told Spencer to watch how fast Brian will go when there's some food around. I opened the box. I showed Brian my dad's lettuce. And – Pshowwww! That snail was off faster than Usain Bolt! We timed Brian and he made it from one side of his shoebox all the way to the other in LESS THAN FOUR MINUTES – so that got me thinking if thousands of people will pay good money to watch Usain Bolt get crowned Fastest Man on Earth, how much do you think they'd pay to see Brian get crowned as Fastest Snail on Earth? Millions, right.

If you think I'm on to a winner here, plz GBTM soon, then I can tell Mr Forbes our school won't be getting that visit from the bailiffs in September.

Otherwise, you could always send us a cheque for £7,000 if that's easier for you.

Good luck and have fun.

Harry Riddles

From Harry **to** Grandma
Subject: Fun Run
26 April 19:05 GMT

Dear O Most Wondrous Grandma –

I have a fun run coming up at the w/e. It's like six miles – which BTW, is more than I've ever run, but me and Dingbat have been looking at the course and we've decided this is a great opportunity to kill two birds with one stone. So I'm pretty confident I'll finish. Will you sponsor me?

BTW, if I get Lord Sir Alan Sugar to come to our school, do you want to come over and meet him? Mum says you think he's hot.

Love

Harry xxx

From Grandma **to** Harry
Subject: Snails
27 April 07:14 CEST

Dear Harry,

Of course I will sponsor you. Five
euros a mile – is that OK? (I'll
make it ten if you can get Lord
Sugar to come to your school.)

Love u lots.

Grandma xxx

BTW – Mum tells me you are worried Brian will
not have enough competition for your Snail Racing
World Championship – which is a BRILLIANT
scheme. Have you thought of using slugs instead?

From Harry **to** Grandma
Subject: Slugs
27 April 07.31 GMT

Dear O Most Wondrous Grandma –

No offence, but I don't think a slug could keep up with Brian. Plus, it's the Snail Racing World Championships, not the Slug *and* Snail Racing World Championships. So I'm going to say no to slugs, but thanks anyway.

Lotsa love

Harry xxx

From Harry **to** Charley
Subject: Mum
27 April 19:21 GMT

Cuz –

This is what I found outside my bedroom door this morning.

Today's Wi-Fi =

1) Make yr bed.
2) Clean up in the kitchen after you make yrself a sandwich.
3) Vacuum downstairs.

If yr father is NOT here, I can NOT run this house without yr help!!!

STAY CONNECTED!!!

Mum :)

So Mum has turned the Wi-Fi off to get me and my sister to help her more. But my sister says she shouldn't have to do any chores, cos she needs to spend ALL her free time in her room studying for her GCSEs. But since when does studying mean talking to Ricky for like three hours every night? Good news is that when I FINALLY finished my chores and FINALLY got given the Wi-Fi password I downloaded WoZ RUN! Which, BTW, is so IN-CREDIBLE!!!

From Harry **to** Charley
Subject: eBay
1 May 21:20 GMT

Cuz –

You know what I found out today? Kids can sell
their World of Zombies RUN! accounts on eBay for
like thousands of pounds! I'm gonna be rich!

Anyway, we have our run tomorrow and Bigstock
is already on my case, saying I'm never gonna
finish, cos I can't bring my bicycle, and if I don't
have a bicycle, I'll never make it, cos I'm a gamer
and I sit on my rear and don't do any exercise and
blah, blah, blah.

And you know something? He may be right but
I wasn't gonna take any of that garbage, so I bet

him I'd finish the run and if I lost I'd help him with his maths. But if I WON, then he'd have to run ALL THE WAY BACK. He took the bet but what I didn't tell him was that I'm taking my dog, cos he has energy TO BURN. I'm just hoping he'll pull me all the way to Padstow.

BTW, don't forget you said you'd sponsor me three bucks if I made it.

From Harry **to** Charley
Subject: Fun Run
3 May 17:05 GMT

Cuz –

You can keep your three bucks. Taking the dog was maybe not my best idea.

From Charley **to** Harry
Subject: Fun Run
3 May 10:10 MTZ

Why? U lose him?

From Harry **to** Charley
Subject: Fun Run
3 May 17:14 GMT

Almost. In fact, there's an outside chance I still might, but I don't want to think about that right now, cos I got other stuff to worry about.

From Charley **to** Harry
Subject: Fun Run
3 May 10:15 MTZ

What r u talking about?

From Harry **to** Charley
Subject: Fun Run
3 May 17:20 GMT

OK, so basically we get down to the trail and when Bigstock sees Dingbat, he says having a dog pull me is cheating and yadda, yadda, yadda but I'm not listening cos I have my phone out and for like the first time since I downloaded WoZ RUN! My activity bar is going completely NUTS! 600 metres down the trail is a LURKER ARMY of zombies hiding out behind some trees. So I don't wait for

Miss Bradshawe to set us on our way, I'm like, "Gotta go! See ya!" And me and the dog start running.

Almost immediately, I see this family coming towards me on their bicycles and they have a dog. I pull Dingbat in on his lead, the family cycle past, their dog goes nuts, but they get past without any trouble with my dog. But all the zombies have now mysteriously disappeared from my tracker bar, so I'm starting to wonder if my game is kind of glitchy. But Dingbat is still pulling like a train, so he's making my run a LOT easier (and faster).

Well, then this other family come cycling up the trail towards me and I see they have a large golden retriever on a lead. I think I'd better be careful, cos my dog LOVES golden retrievers. So I shorten the lead and just then

BOOOOOOOMMMMM! My tracker bar goes CRAZY!
I've got Biter zombies coming at me from
some bushes in front, from some bushes
behind, coming out the river – I mean they
are like EVERYWHERE and I can't run. I have
to battle! It was like OMG FINALLY! THIS IS SO
GREATTTTTTTTTTTTTTTTTTTTTTTTTTTTTTTTTTT
TT!!!!!!!!!!

Anyway, I get into this HUMONGOUS firenado fight, and I'm like rake trailing and monkey bombing and swiping right and it's like THE COOLEST GAME I've ever played! But then I hear Dingbat barking and he's not where he should be. So my alarm bells start ringing, I look up from my screen, and that's when I see Dingbat running straight towards the lady with the big retriever. When this woman sees my dog racing towards her dog, she FALLS OFF her bicycle. For no reason at all!

Then things go downhill FAST, cos when she falls off her two kids crash into her and they FALL OFF. And when the two kids fall off, the dad, who is bringing up the rear of this train wreck, has to swing out wide to avoid running them over and he knocks over another family on bicycles going the OTHER way and they all FALL OFF. So basically my gaming was pretty much responsible for a ten-person pile-up on the Camel Trail.

And that wasn't even the worst of it. When the lady crashes, she drops the lead and her dog – I think it was called Riley – BOLTS. Him and Dingbat run up the bike trail, barking, causing more trouble as MORE families fall off their bicycles. And that's when Bigstock runs up next to me and says, "Nice work Harry! Next time leave the dog at home, you little moron!"

Anyway, I go over to say I'm sorry, but this woman is so mad she wants my name, my address, my telephone number and all this other stuff, cos she says my dog's a menace and we need to be punished and fined and I don't know what. She said if we were in London, she'd have MY DOG TAKEN TO THE DOG POUND!!!

Well I wasn't gonna let anybody take Dingbat off to the dog pound, so I picked him up and ran him all the way back to Mum's car before that woman could cause me more trouble. When I told Mum what happened, she said she'd talk to the woman and apologise. But that didn't help AT ALL, cos the woman told Mum she wanted to call the police because dogs are not allowed off the lead, and my dog's a menace and blah, blah, blah. Mum tried to explain that I had been distracted by my excellent new video game and it was just one of those unfortunate things. But that was like putting fuel on the fire, cos the woman then starts lecturing Mum about spending more time parenting her kid and less time passing the duty on to a stupid video game and a wild dog.

Anyway, when Mum got back
to the car, she said it's time
I learnt to put other things
first in life. If that wasn't bad
enough, when we finally go
to Padstow to meet up with
everybody, Bigstock said he had
a ton of maths homework waiting
for me in his dad's Land Rover.

I hate fun runs.

What's going on in Denver? You guys winning all
your lacrosse games?

GBTM soon.

Harry

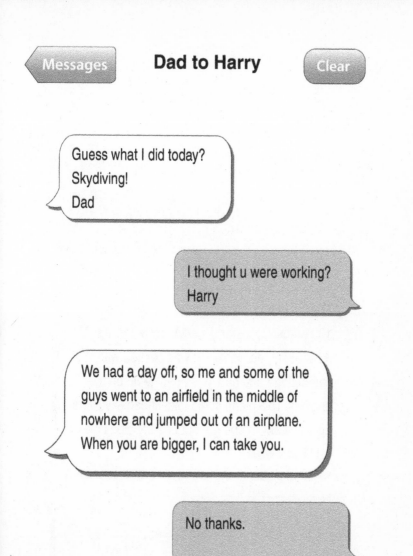

Guess what I did today?
Skydiving!
Dad

I thought u were working?
Harry

We had a day off, so me and some of the guys went to an airfield in the middle of nowhere and jumped out of an airplane. When you are bigger, I can take you.

No thanks.

It was LOTS of fun.

Did u get any pictures?

They said no pictures unless you pay them 100 euros. So instead, here's my plane. It's a twin-engined Dornier. It was painted with camouflage and had these cool teeth on the engines. This plane could take fifteen skydivers up in the sky in one go. But I nearly didn't make it. U know why?

So?

So when I got there I was too heavy with eating all that film truck food. So this is what I had to do…

Sit in a baking hot car for like an hour and sweat off the pounds. And then I could do this...

Oh – and I learnt this secret handshake up in the plane. Only skydivers know this shake, but I can tell you, cos you're my kid.

Skydivers' handshake!

So next time you give Walnut a high five – show him one of these, cos they're pretty cool. What do you think?

I think u should just come home.

You don't like my drawings? I did 'em just for you on the iPad.

U know what Jessica told me today? Her mum is sending her off to boarding school, so I'm probably never going to see her again.

I'm sorry, Harry.

I know. It really sucks.

Well, maybe the way to think about it is kind of like this...

What's that?

That fish with the hoodie in the middle? That's you. All around you are some very pretty fishes, cos there are plenty more fish in the sea.

Jessica is not a fish but she is pretty.

I know.

Plus, u know what else Jessica says? She says I play too many video games and I should quit cos they just mess everything up and make people fall off their bicycles. I said I'll quit playing video games if you tell your mum you don't want to go to boarding school...

What did she say?

No.

From Dad **to** Harry
Subject: Email from Mr Forbes
19 May 21:23 CEST

My kid,

Have you seen this?

From Mr Malcolm Forbes **to** Mr & Mrs W. Riddles
(and 120 others)
Subject: Our school
17 May 09:15 GMT

Dear Parents-Against-The-Closure-of-Mount-Joseph's-School,

Firstly, a big thank-you for all your kind wishes for a speedy recovery. I'm fully recovered now and very much looking forward to our annual school trip to London next week.

I'd also like to give a big shout out to Years 4, 5 & 6 for a magnificent £204 raised on the recent Fun Run from Wadebridge to Padstow! Well done to you and well done Ed Bigstock for getting that ball rolling! An excellent effort all round!

As I'm sure you all know, we still have a mountain to climb to keep Mount Joseph's open, but I am quietly optimistic that with your continued support, we can keep chipping away and will have an excellent chance of succeeding!

With that in mind I would like to invite you all to 'An Afternoon With Olympic Legend Sir Peter Van Horne'. Sir Peter will be spending Saturday 28th June with Jessica MacDougal and her mother Joan and their horse Thunderbolt for an afternoon of riding, time trialling, and personal one-on-one expert tuition (for a small fee!) So for all of you horse lovers at Mount Joseph's, here is an incredible opportunity to have a lesson, picture, and/or conversation with living Olympic legend Sir Peter. During our school summer fête, we will also be offering a number of other extremely attractive, fun-filled activities, so put the date in your diary and we look forward to seeing you all then!

Kind regards,

Malcolm Forbes

From Harry **to** Dad
Subject: Mr Forbes email
20 May 11:16 GMT

Pups,

Ed has been bragging about that letter every minute he gets a chance. He even told Mr Forbes that if he's still in his job in September, it will all be because of HIM!

How come you can write to me during lesson time? Are you at home sick?
Dad

No, I'm on the train to London. It's my school trip, remember?
Harry

Can I call you later?

I don't think Mr Forbes likes us talking to our parents when we're away.

Well, if you need anything, I'm here. Enjoy yourself and try not to get into any trouble.

From Harry **to** Pequod Games Labs (press@ pequodgameslabs.com)
Subject: Zombies in Cornwall
21 May 11:01 GMT

Dear Pequod Games, makers of the incredible and amazing World of Zombies RUN! game, hi there!

I've been playing your game for a while now, but I have a question for you guys. Where are all the CRAWLER zombies at? I've been where you'd think Crawler zombies hang out – like Tesco and Morrisons, where there's LOTS AND LOTS of DEAD MEAT, but I didn't find any. I even got my mum to drive me to the butcher shop in Wadebridge, cos they have real pig bodies hanging on hooks in the window. Still nothing. Why's that?

Good news is, I just read some Reddit posts that

says London has more zombies than ANY other place in the whole of the UK, so this school trip could be a GREAT opportunity for me to build a HUGE score, which I need if I want to sell it.

OMG, gotta go! My tracker bar is telling me there is HIGH ZOMBIE ACTIVITY in the buffet car next door!

From Harry **to** Pequod Games Lab (press@ pequodgameslab.com)
Subject: Antivirals
21 May 11:58 GMT

Dear Pequod Games, it's me again! Hi there!

OK, now I could be in big trouble. I went into the buffet car and it was rammed with Biters. So we get into this incredible firenado fight but this makes some business guy mad cos he spills his coffee. So while I'm saying sorry to him, a bunch of Lurkers start trying to sneak up behind me. I see them on my battle screen, spin round, unleash a firestorm of monkey bombs, but their DEATH screams make this little baby start CRYING in his chair. Before I can do anything, the baby's mum tries to grab my phone! It turns out, she was

even more dangerous than a car full of ZOMBIES. It was because of her that I got bitten by some Roamer – trying to get my phone! So now the clock's ticking to find a Cure Station, or three weeks of hardcore gaming is GONE.

Good news is, our train arrives at Paddington station at 12:06. My avatar will die at 12:15 – unless I find some antivirals and revitalise. That gives me nine minutes. The Reddit posts say that the Paddington Bear statue at Paddington station has everything I need. Problem is, I've googled it and the statue is on the east side of the station and we arrive on the west side. But you know what? Maybe I should just go and talk to Mr Forbes.

OK. I just talked to Mr Forbes and told him how much I really want to go and see the Paddington Bear statue. He said he never knew I was a secret

Paddington Bear fan (I'm not), but now that he knows, we can make a quick detour and get some photos! So we're going to see the bear before we get on the Underground to go to our hotel. And if it means me cuddling up to a statue and having my photo taken, I figure that's a sacrifice worth making if I can revitalise and keep playing and slaying!

Good news is tomorrow we're going to the Tower of London on a big red bus and I know the Roamers have made the Tower a zombie base, which means there will be an epic BATTLE (and HUGE SCORE). Afterwards,

I'm gonna try and get Mr Forbes to take us to the Bank of England on Threadneedle Street and capture some zombie bullion, cos that place is gonna be packed full of it. But I know that even if I build a HUGE score, I'm not going to get to the end of the game before we get back to Cornwall. What worries me is: will I be able to find Not So Normal Norm in Cornwall to have my Final Battle? I can't sell my game until I've beaten Norm.

Plz GBTM soon.

Thanks a lot.

Harry
harryriddles@gmail.com

I know I shouldn't be bothering you, but how's London? You having a good time?
Dad

It's OK.
Harry

Not having fun?

I have to write to some dude and apologise – which is kind of embarrassing, TBH.

What did you do?

I'll tell you when I get home.
I gotta go. Bye.

From Harry **to** Joe Greene (press@
theresonlyonejimmygrimble.com)
Subject: Your show
22 May 07:42 GMT

Dear Joe Greene, writer of the hit West End
musical, *There's Only One Jimmy Grimble*, hi there!

First off, I'm REALLY sorry about what happened
last night. My teacher said you probably won't
even get told about it, but I should write anyway,
cos it's good manners.

To be honest, I didn't want to. Partly, cos I've got
enough on my plate with everything going on at
my school, and partly because you're probably
never going to understand why I had to go and
hunt some Crawler zombies, when I'm sitting in
the theatre watching your amazing show. But the

truth is, I've been looking for these zombies for like WEEKS now, and I knew I had to hunt them when I could, or I may NEVER get another chance – even if that kid Jimmy is singing some song about his magic boots.

So when I get the alert on my phone in my pocket, I tell my friend Jessica that I have to go to the bathroom. I grab my backpack, cos it has my inhaler, my antihistamine pills, and all this other stuff my mum wanted me to keep with me at all times in case I get chesty, then I squeeze past Bulmer, Bigstock, and Mr Forbes, and RUN for the bathroom (cos these guys can sometimes just disappear).

Anyway, when I get in there, I put my pack down by the basin, I get my phone out to scope the bathroom and almost immediately they start coming at ME. I mean, there are Crawlers crawling

out from underneath the toilet cubicles, coming
over the top of the toilet doors – the bathroom
was a nest FULL of 'em!

So I get in this HUMONGOUS battle, but I only have like three monkey bombs and zero spinning firenados in my arsenal, cos I haven't had time to re-arm and power up, so I use my monkey bombs, but now I'm out of ammo and the Crawlers are beginning to SURROUND me, so I have to get out of there and get out of there FAST, or I'm DEAD MEAT.

I jump over one Crawler. I pull the door open. I get out before I get bitten and when I finally get back to my seat my heart's racing, but I'm pumped, cos I just made a HUGE score. So I sit back and watch Jimmy and that moron Johnny Two Dogs sing some song called "I'm Your New Dad!" Next thing I know, the fire bell starts ringing, and some guy rushes out on stage and tells us we all have to evacuate the building IMMEDIATELY!

We get up to file out the theatre, but it's a bun fight in the aisle, cos the adults start pushing and shoving each other to get out as fast as they can, cos they're all a bunch of cowards.

Anyway, we make it out a side door and there are now like TONS of people on the street, cos it's a busy night on Shaftesbury Avenue. So Mr Forbes is trying to get us together to do a headcount, when the police and the fire brigade and all these other cars with flashing blue lights screech up outside the main entrance. That's when my friend Jessica looks at me and says, "Where's your backpack, Harry?"

We don't have to wait long to find out. The manager comes out the front door of the theatre and he's got my pack in his hand. He looks at Mr Forbes and asks him if he has a student called H.W. Riddles.

Well, Bigstock lets out this enormous GROAN and pretty soon everybody on the street knew it was all my fault that nobody could see the end of your brilliant show. The manager asked me why I left my pack in the bathroom. I didn't think it was a good idea to tell him about the Crawlers, so I shrugged, but Bigstock tells the manager that I was probably hunting zombies, cos that's all I've been doing since we got to London.

And basically, Bigstock was right. But I have to build a big score or I can't sell the game for a lot of money and save my school. Anyway, we really loved your musical. I'm guessing Jimmy has a happy ending? If so, he's doing a lot better than me, cos I'm in heaps of trouble.

I'm really sorry for all the trouble I caused. Mr Forbes said I had a lot of apologies to make to all the other disappointed theatregoers. Luckily, I don't have all their names and addresses (but I think Mr Forbes is working on that).

Good luck and have fun.

Harry Riddles

From Harry **to** Charley
Subject: The National Lacrosse Championship Final
22 May 07:50 GMT

Dear Cuz –

I know you've kinda given up writing to me, cos you got your big lacrosse tournament later today. But I'm in London with my school, which, BTW, isn't going as well as I'd hoped, but we're going to go sightseeing today and maybe go to Platform 9 3/4 at King's Cross station (where you can catch the Hogwarts Express) – if we have time.

I know I won't hear back from you, but do me a favour, kick some Pennsylvania rear for me, OK?

Harry

What's going on, squid? U get to King's Cross?
U going to Hogwarts?
Charley

Ha ha. No.
Harry

So what's it like?

It's OK.

That's all? I thought you'd LOVE that place!

I just told my friend Jessica that it would be really cool if me and her could get on the Hogwart's Express, but she said she didn't want to go to Hogwarts next term, she was happy going off to her new school, so that kinda sucks.

Chin up, Smurf. Can't be ALL bad.

It isn't. In fact, King's Cross is like being in LURKER ZOMBIE HEAVEN!!!

So what r u waiting for? Merc 'em dude.

Give me a call when you are on the train. Or if you don't want to call, text. I'll see you at the station. Love u.
Mum xxx

Hi Mum, I ran out of battery cos my game is a BATTERY KILLER, so I went to the bathroom to plug in and recharge, but when I came out, Mr Forbes was pulling his hair out, cos he didn't know where I'd got to, and now I think we might be late for our train.
Harry

What on earth are you doing going to the bathroom without telling Mr Forbes? No wonder he's pulling his hair out. Poor Mr Forbes! I thought I made it very clear that you were to stay close to the group and not wander off playing that game!

I know.

When you get home, we're going to have to have a little talk about your gaming.

Uh-oh.

From Harry **to** Mary Berry (mary@maryberry.co.uk)
Subject: School bake off
1 June 18:05 GMT

Dear Mary Berry, *Great British Bake Off* Queen, hi
there!

My mum and sister really loved your TV show
and said basically that it was one of the worst
decisions ever made in television history to move
your show to a different home without you, cos
they loved seeing you on the TV.

TBH, I never watched your show, cos I prefer
hunting zombies to baking cakes, but my zombie
hunting days are on ice, since my dad got home
and my parents decided they wanted to put my
phone in gamer jail after what happened at King's
Cross station. I've tried telling them this isn't

about me gaming, this is about me trying to SAVE MY SCHOOL, but they said playing video games will NOT save Mount Joseph's, but a successful bake off MIGHT. And it's time for me to have a digital detox, take some time out from gaming, and help them try and do something positive for my school.

Well, I know they are my parents and they should know best, but you know what? They don't. If I could get to the end of WoZ RUN! then beat Norm, I could make A LOT OF MONEY!!! My sister told me that if I keep on arguing with my dad about my need to keep playing WoZ, we probably won't see him for another six months, cos he'll just take another job on a movie and go off on location somewhere, cos my gaming will drive him crazy. Then it will be MY FAULT that he's not living with us.

So what could I do? I had to give in. Now my phone is in jail (which, BTW, is at the bottom of Dad's sock drawer) and if we don't do well at the school fête on the 28th, I don't know what's going to happen, cos my hands are now tied.

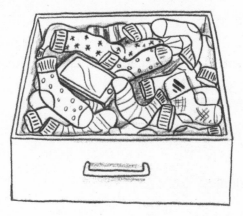

Which is why I'm writing to you. Me and the kids in my class have sold most of the bake off tickets to the parents, but we're still like three thousand pounds short, so we need to sell a LOT more tickets to random strangers. Jessica said that unless we get somebody famous like you to come to our school fête, we'll fail, cos snail racing and a ride on old Thunderbolt doesn't have the same pulling power as getting a big star like you to stand at one of our stalls and bake some of your delicious cakes.

So will you have a think about it, please? Thanks a lot!

Good luck and have fun.

Harry Riddles

From Harry **to** Charley
Subject: Home
04 June 16:54 GMT

Dear Cuz –

Dad's been home for like a whole week now
which, BTW, is really great, but he said we may
have to MOVE if we all want to live together again,
cos he's found a new job teaching down in Falmouth.
When I told Jessica she said it could be a good
thing for me, because then maybe I'd be nearer my
friends, cos I'll be closer to my new school. I didn't
say anything, but her idea really sucks. I don't want
to move anywhere. I love my house.

Anyway, Mum and Dad are keeping my phone in
jail until my dad goes back to Spain for one last
time, so now I make Dad play backgammon with

me every night when I come home from school. I pretty much kick his rear, cos he can't roll the dice like I can. I'm kind of hoping if I beat him enough, he'll get fed up with losing and give me my phone back earlier, cos he's a bad loser. But we'll see.

BTW, you know what's really weird? Me and Bigstock are starting to hang out (a little). I've been helping him with his maths, cos he's got to take some test to go to this school that his dad wants him to go to. Jessica said the reason he's suddenly being a LOT nicer to everybody (including me) is that his dad just left his mum, so he's like, confused. Let's just hope he stays confused until the end of term.

Anyway, we have the school fête coming up and I'm really pumped to take Brian. He's probably in the best shape of his life, because after I play backgammon with my dad, we get Brian down from my room and train him on the kitchen table. Mum isn't a big fan, but Dad said if we want to breed a champion, we all have to make some sacrifices. Mum said eating dinner on a kitchen table covered in snail slime is not a sacrifice she or my sister want to make. Even if we are breeding champions and the table has been wiped with a cloth.

What's up with you?

GBTM soon.

Harry

CHAPTER TWELVE
MAGIC BOOTS

From Harry **to** Dad
Subject: Letters
17 June 20:01 GMT

Pups,

Look what I just found in my mail.

From Joe Greene joegreene@gmail.com **to** Harry
(harryriddles1@gmail.com)
Subject: There's Only One Jimmy Grimble
17 June 10:21 GMT

Dear Harry,

I'm sorry not to have responded earlier, but thank you for your kind note. I completely understand the need to hunt those elusive Crawler zombies when they appear. As you say, they are an extremely nasty, and very tricky bunch to locate and kill. In fact, should it have been me surrounded and about to be eaten, I would certainly have left my backpack in that bathroom. So do not worry. And now that you have told me we have a small, lethal zombie army hiding in the rest room, I have an excellent reason to leave my office and go and watch my show for the millionth time. So thank you for that hot tip, and if you and any of your schoolmates ever wish for some more tickets to see the whole musical (hopefully without further interruptions), then please ask and I will arrange for tickets to be made available at no cost (and perhaps we can swop notes on the whereabouts of Not So Normal Norm?).

Best wishes,

Joe Greene

From Dad **to** Harry
Subject: Crawlers
17 June 21:03 CEST

Who is Joe Greene and what are Crawlers?

Joe Greene is like a really cool writer who wrote the musical *There's Only One Jimmy Grimble*. Crawlers are zombies in my World of Zombies RUN! Game. Joe Greene LOVES WoZ RUN! (Plus Joe Greene is a real ADULT!)
Harry

Are you sure?
Dad

U don't have to be a kid to play video games, Dad. U should try it.

Not in a million years.

From Harry **to** Joe Greene (joegreene@gmail.com)
Subject: Magic Boots
18 June 18:20 GMT

Dear Joe Greene, hi again!

Thank you for your letter. I'm really sorry to
bother you again, but when we were talking
about your musical in class, Mr Forbes asked us
all what we liked best about your story. I told him
the funniest thing for me was that kid who lived
up on the same floor as Jimmy on the council
estate. He lived in the flat next door to Melanie
Morrison and he was always heaving stuff over
the balcony wall – like that TV he tossed down
into the car park when Gorgeous Gordon Burley
and Johnny Two Dogs were plotting to steal
Jimmy's magic football boots. When the

TV EXPLODED and made them jump, it was like HILARIOUS! A little later we discover that this kid is so naughty cos he's really mad at his parents for getting divorced. That's why he does all the crazy stuff.

Well, there's a kid in my class called Ed Bigstock, who is kind of like that. He doesn't chuck TVs over the balcony, but I'll bet he'd like to if he could get away with it cos he can be naughty, too, given half a chance. His parents are getting divorced and he used to be a bully, but now he's a lot nicer, which is pretty crazy, right? TBH, I wish they'd got divorced sooner, then my life at school would have been a LOT easier.

Anyway, I'm writing cos my friend Bulmer said he thought Jimmy Grimble was based on a TRUE STORY. He said those magic boots really exist and if we had a pair our school would stay open, cos those boots can make dreams come true. I don't know if I believe him, but we're running out of time to make the money we need to keep our school open, so I thought it was worth asking.

Do they?

Thanks a lot for reading this.

Good luck and have fun.

Harry
harryriddles1@gmail.com

From Joe Greene **to** Harry Riddles
Subject: Magic Boots
19 June 07:12 GMT

Dear Harry,

I am really sorry to hear about your school's financial problems. Unfortunately, the magic boots are NOT real. I made them up, but thanks for giving me the idea for my sequel. I've been scratching my head for months.

Best wishes,

Joe Greene

From Harry **to** Joe
Subject: Magic Boots
19 June 07:15 GMT

Dear Joe,

When you've written it, can we come see that one, too?

Harry

From Joe Greene **to** Harry
Subject: Magic Boots
19 June 07:17 GMT

Dear Harry,

Of course.

BTW – I'm now at Level 15 and wondering where to find Not So Normal Norm. You have any ideas?

Joe

From Harry **to** Joe
Subject: Not So Normal Norm
19 June 07:31 GMT

Dear Joe,

My phone is STILL in gamer jail, so I can't play right now. Plus, nobody on Reddit has found Norm in Cornwall. But if I hear where he is, I'll let you know. OK? BTW, if anybody asks me what I want to be when I get older, I'm gonna tell 'em I want to be a writer just like you. Then I can play video games ALL DAY LONGGGGGGGGGGGGGGGGGGGGGGGGGGGGGGG GGGGGGG!!!

Harry

From Harry **to** Mr Forbes
Subject: Magic Boots
20 June 19:04 GMT

Dear Mr Forbes,

I didn't see you at school today – are you OK? I hope you didn't fall off your bicycle again, but I thought you might like to see this. It's from that guy you made me write to. Good news is, he's not mad at me for the backpack thing (phew).

See you tomorrow.

Harry

From Mr Forbes **to** Harry
Subject: Magic Boots
20 June 23:04 GMT

Dear Harry,

Thank you for those letters, which I have now read
with great interest. I am hoping I can persuade
Mr Greene to come down for our sports day as a
Friend of Mount Joseph's to give out some prizes
and a little speech to our Leavers, because he
might have a few wise words to help you kids on
your journey through school! Well done, Harry!

Mr Forbes

CHAPTER THIRTEEN
A DEATH IN THE FAMILY

Dear Cuz –

Today, our school fête was marred by personal
tragedy. When I woke up this morning I thought
this was going to be Brian's Big Date with Destiny.
After weeks of hard training, he was going to earn
his just rewards as a world-beating athlete, take
his place in snail racing history, and make the
school a ton of money.

Instead, he got caught up in the middle of a HUGE
argument between Mrs Bigstock and Mr Bigstock.
The fight ended when Mrs Bigstock pushed Mr
Bigstock and he fell back and squashed Brian. I
was gutted and, TBH, pretty mad with both of

them, but there was
nothing I could do.
Dad tried to make
things better by
saying we can give
what's left of Brian
a Viking funeral,
and put him in a
burning matchbox
and send him down
the stream at the
bottom of our
garden. But I've
thought about it
and I think Brian
would prefer it if
we shot him up
into space on a
firework that

goes BOOOOOOOOOOOOOOOOOOOOOMMM!!!
Cos he's an astronaut.

What do you think?

Harry

From Charley **to** Harry
Subject: Brian
28 June 12:56 MTZ

I think boom!!!

From Charley **to** Harry
Subject: The end
28 June 13:01 MTZ

BTW, anybody else come to a nasty and grisly end?

From Harry **to** Charley

Subject: Nasty end

29 June 20:20 GMT

Well, Sir Peter Van Horne fell off old Thunderbolt (predictably) when the horse got spooked by a car backfiring. Jessica's mum had to run him down to the A&E in Plymouth. Other than that, no. But the good news is, the Riddles twins showed a LOT of athletic promise – which really pleased my dad. They crawled away with the winning prize in the Toddler Triathlon. Unfortunately that victory was disputed because somebody told Mrs Farmer that

Charlotte's new boyfriend, Ricky, had given the twins an unfair advantage when he stamped on the training harness of their number one rival. Apparently, this other baby was unbelievably quick and would have beaten the twins had Ricky not interfered. So he got the prize, not the twins – which was a bit disappointing for my dad.

Anyway, my birthday is coming up next week and if I can get my phone back, maybe I can finish the game before we run out of time with the school, cos I don't think the parents or Mr Forbes have got any more brilliant money-spinning schemes and we're running out of time.

Going to bed now.

Night, Cuz.

Harry

CHAPTER FOURTEEN
BIRTHDAY BOY

From Harry **to** Sir Philip Green (spg@arcadia.com)
Subject: Birthdays
4 July 20:04 GMT

Dear Sir Philip Green, party animal and owner of
my sister's favourite high street store, hi there!

I'm gonna be eleven years old next week and
when I told my mum I didn't know what kind
of party to have, she said I should write to you,
cos you throw the best parties around. I think
she thought I wouldn't bother writing cos she
was poking fun at me, but when I googled you I
thought, you know what? Mum's got it right again!
Look at all the incredibly famous people who
turned up to your party. Superstars like Kate Moss,
Leonardo DiCaprio and Simon Cowell! If you can
get all those guys to come to your party, then you
must be doing something right.

So my first question is: is it true that you rented
a jet for your friends and paid Stevie Wonder,
Robbie Williams, Michael Bublé, the Beach Boys
and I don't know who else to come out and sing
for you? Is that a deal-breaker? When I talked to
my mum, she said she'd take me and my friends
over to Port Isaac in the back of our old pick-up
and hopefully get the Fisherman's Friends to sing
me "Happy Birthday". I know the Friends are good
but they are not Robbie Williams.

I also read that you got your guests to play beach
volleyball and then treated them to some special
hamburgers of Kobe beef, which costs like 50
pounds A BURGER. Mum and Dad won't go for
that idea, but they might take us paintballing and
then on to Alice in Burgerland. Her burgers cost
about five pounds each, which is a lot for round
here, but they're really tasty and she doesn't

mind how much ketchup you use.

One thing I don't understand is why you made all your guests wear clothing with your initials and your age on. What's that all about? I asked Mum if we need to do something like this and she said we could, but we're not going to, cos it's kind of weird (and very expensive). Then she told me to forget having a beach party with rivers and rivers of champagne, cos we're kids and Tango is better for us, which was fine by me. But thanks anyway for sharing your great day online and I'll let you now how mine goes.

Good luck and have fun.

Harry

Dear Jessica, I know I said we would be going paintballing but we can't cos my dad went out on the boat yesterday to fish for lobster and he got three fingers trapped in Chris's winch. He's OK, but he doesn't want to go paintballing. Will you still come over?
Harry

Of course I will! Is yr dad gonna be ok?
Jessica

He says he'll be fine. BTW, I know my mum told your mum that I'd written to Sir Philip Green for some party tips, but getting Robbie Williams to sing for me is not going to be one of them. Sorry.

I don't care.

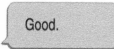

Good.

Have you had a good day?

Uh-huh. Mum decorated our kitchen, so when I came down for breakfast there were LOTS of balloons on the kitchen table, and glitter, and presents, and a big shiny banner above the kitchen window that said, HAPPY BIRTHDAY, HARRY! Which was like really cool. Plus, my sister stayed over at her friend's house, so there were no birthday wedgies from her. And Mum made me lots and lots of homemade pancakes – which was great!

Jessica to Harry

Did you get a lot of presents?
Jessica

I got a diver's watch. A super cool gamer mouse (the best one ever made. It's called the Razor Death Adder – but you probably don't want to hear about it). Plus I got a surf robie so I can get changed down on the beach. You should get yr mum to get you one. They are really cool. See ya at twelve!
Harry

From Charley **to** Harry
Subject: Birthdays!
11 July 11:11 MTZ

Squid,

Whussssssssupppppppppppppp???? Happy
birthday little man! U havin' a good day?
What's going on? Lemme know.

Charley

From Harry **to** Charley
Subject: My birthday
11 July 20:05 GMT

I had a good day.

That's it? Doesn't sound like a good day.
Charley

Hmm.
Harry

What's the matter?

Nothing.

Doesn't sound like nothing. What's going on, H?

Well, the good news is I grew an inch and a half this term so I don't have to go and live with the Borrowers!

That's great! So what's the bad news?

I had to say goodbye to Jessica. She's going to boarding school next term, so I probably won't see her again. She said we can email each other and text and Skype and it will be just like we were at school together. I said it won't.

I thought term doesn't finish for another two weeks?

It doesn't but her mum is taking her out early, cos they are going to America so she can audition for some new TV show, cos she wants to be a famous actress.

I'm sorry, Harry.

Me 2. I told her to have a nice time at her new school, and if she gets famous to remember us at Mount Joseph's. She said she will. Then she got in the car and they left.

No goodbye kiss?

I might have got one.

Well, that's nice, right?

I'm gonna go to bed now.

CHAPTER FIFTEEN
DAB

From Harry **to** Charley
Subject: My new school
18 July 21:24 GMT

Dear Cuz –

Roseland High School. OMG, what a day! When Mum came into my room to get me up to go and have my Reception Day, I said basically I was sick and not going ANYWHERE, cos I didn't want to get out of bed. Some people had come to our house yesterday and told Dad that they wanted to buy it, but I don't want to leave. I figured if I stayed in bed, then we can't move.

But then I found an email from Jessica in America, which was really funny. When Mum heard me laughing she said if I'm well enough to laugh, I'm well enough to go to Reception Day. End of.

Anyway, we get in the car and we drive all the way down to the Roseland (which, BTW, is like MILES away) and I've got butterflies, cos I can't stop thinking about what happened to Walnut when he went up to big school and they locked him in a garbage dumpster for the day. But Mum says this isn't gonna happen at this school, cos it's a nice school. Mum said I had nothing to be nervous about, cos she is hoping to get a JOB at the school starting in September. I think she thought this would make me feel better, but it just made me feel WORSE.

Anyway, we get down there and while we're waiting for the headmistress I notice this other kid in Reception who's even smaller than me, which I thought was a good sign. Then the lady at the desk asked if any of us kids liked to play video games?

Well, every hand in the room shoots up (including the girls) and she goes, "I think you'll like what our headmistress has lined up for you kids today!" So now I'm starting to think this place isn't so bad. Then you know what happened? The kid who is smaller than me looks over and says, "You play World of Zombies?" I tell him I do and he's like, "You any good?" I tell him I'm MLG (Major League Gamer) and he asks what name I use online. So I go, I'm Kid Zombie. You know what he does? He dabs me! Do you have that in America? You put your arms out to one side while you turn your head the other way? Every kid in my school does it. That and the bottle flick. Anyway, I dab him back. Then he tells me that him and me have played a LOT online, because his online name is darkassassin300. So he's the very same kid I played in my one v one death match at activity camp! His real name is Lucas.

From that moment on, I felt a whole LOT happier about this school, cos I had made a new friend. Me and him spent the rest of the day hanging out talking World of Zombies. He hasn't downloaded the WoZ RUN! Game cos his mum and dad haven't given him one of their old smart phones, but he's hoping to get one next week.

I told Lucas at lunch about the problems my school is having and how it might close unless I can get to the end of WoZ RUN! And he said basically he'd help me find Norm, which was really cool. So, fingers crossed that all works out. If it doesn't at least I got somebody new to play with, cos Walnut is leaving for Australia next week. What's going on with you?

GBTM soon,

Harry

From Charley **to** Harry
Subject: Stuff
19 July 12:05 MTZ

I'm home and we're all getting pretty excited about this summer. Dad says he's booked us the tickets so we're definitely coming to Europe to stay with Grandma. I'm going to see you in August, Cuz. Then we can teach Grandma how to dab!

From Harry **to** Charley
Subject: Yay!
19 July 20:24 GMT

OMG, Yay!

CHAPTER SIXTEEN

THREE LEGS ARE
BETTER THAN TWO

From Harry **to** Joe Greene, (joe.greene@gmail.com)
Subject: Our school
22 July 20:04 GMT

Dear Joe Greene, hi there (again)!

First off, I want to thank you for giving my school
that amazing cheque for £2,500. Mr Forbes said
that you told him it was the least you could do
after I'd given you such a brilliant idea for your
sequel. Well, I don't know if it's a brilliant idea, but
if it is, I hope it makes you lots of money. So thank
you and thanks for coming down to our sports day
to give out the prizes and make a speech. Nobody
here really thought you would turn up. But I knew
you'd come, cos you're a cool gamer.

TBH, never in a month of Sundays did I imagine a
day when me and Ed Bigstock would be called up

to collect a joint prize for coming second in the three-legged egg and spoon race, cos I've never won any race EVER at Mount Joseph's. And to do it with him was weird, cos he normally tries to push me over. Him choosing me to be his racing partner for the three-legged race, was, I guess, his way of saying thank you for helping him with his maths and sorry for being such a moron for like the last five years. Maybe.

Anyway, the best part of the day for me was when you made your speech about daring to dream the impossible, and how we should harness our fears of the future. Then when you talked about parents and their fears of gaming and gamers like me, and how if they could face their fears and help me win my WoZ game, Mount Joseph's might even stay open, I don't think anybody believed a word you said – until you told them HOW MUCH I could make if I won.

To see every parent there start downloading WoZ RUN! on their phones, to try and help me find Norm so I could sell the game on eBay was, like, so cool. I know most parents HATE gaming and games, but for one minute there, you had them all on my side. Even all the haters. It was totally awesome.

So that was my last ever sports day at Mount Joseph's. I just hope my dad doesn't get any stupid ideas about me becoming inspired to become more sporty, cos that day will never come.

Anyway, I'm home now with my Leavers hoodie on, which is a pretty cool thing, cos it has all the names of my classmates written on it.

When you come down to Cornwall again, please visit. My dad said you might like to talk to his students about writing for the stage and screen. Personally, I'm more interested in Norm. I still can't find him and I don't know if I ever will. I met this new kid who is now my friend and he's looking for him, too, but so far we have no leads. I keep looking on Reddit, but nobody knows where he is. If you hear anything, please let me know.

Thanks again for trying to help, and for giving us SO MUCH money.

Good luck and have fun.

Harry

CHAPTER SEVENTEEN
NOT SO NORMAL
NORM

From Harry **to** Charley
Subject: Not So Normal Norm
28 July 19.41 GMT

Dear Cuz –

5pm today was deadline day for my school
closure. If the remaining shortfall wasn't there
(£2,225), the governors had told some local
developer guy to come and pick up the keys, cos
the doors of Mount Joseph's School would never
be open for kids again.

Funny thing was, I really thought that was it. We'd
lost and there was nothing more anybody could
do. So when my dad said, 'It's a nice day – let's all
go to the beach and have one last family picnic
at our favourite spot before we move,' I thought,
why not? I've tried and tried to find Norm, but

the guy's a no-show. Maybe he doesn't exist in Cornwall. Maybe those gamer guys at Pequod Games Labs are pulling our chain and he's not even MADE!

So we go down to our local beach, which is called Strangles and you can only get to it by walking. It's at the bottom of this cliff and is normally empty even in the middle of summer, because most families don't want the walk. Plus, it's next to this nudist beach. But my mum loves the beach, cos you can take the dog all year round.

Anyway, we go down there with our picnic and we're sitting around talking about my school, when I fire up my phone to see if there might be some kind of sea-zombie-type creature in the ocean. Almost immediately my activity bar goes RED. Not So Normal Norm is NEARBY!!!!!!!!!

I jump to my feet. I move around with my phone.
I locate Norm's approximate location and he's on
the beach next to ours – the NUDIST beach!!!

So I talk to my dad and I explain that he has to
go and battle Norm and SAVE MY SCHOOL! But
my dad said, it must be some kind of technical
error with the algorithms, cos why would Pequod
Games put Norm on a beach full of nudists? What
kind of stupid idea is that?

Luckily, Mum was there and she told Dad that
Mount Joseph's had been a really great school
for me and my sister and here was our chance to
finally give something back and HELP!

Well, Dad didn't like this idea AT ALL, but he
agreed to help, so I carefully explained how
to battle Norm, what bombs to use, when to

swipe left, when to swipe right, when to unleash a spinning firenado, or a monkey bomb, and basically how to kick Norm's rear, but I wasn't sure if he took it all in, cos he's a gamer newbie.

So then it was battle time. Before he went, he made me promise I would never ever make him do this again. Then he climbed over the rocks on to the next beach and found Norm soon afterwards sitting in a cave behind some naked Germans.

Anyway, with my help, Dad beat Norm in an epic battle that had him running up the beach, leaping over rocks, and running into the surf, but eventually he WON. And it was kind of a really big deal for him, cos he ran back to our beach screaming and shouting and jumping up and down that we'd done it! We'd just saved Mount Joseph's!

At 4:58 – two minutes before deadline – Dad called Mr Forbes and told him me and him had the money for the school. Mr Forbes was so happy he started crying.

What a great day!

Harry

CHAPTER SEVENTEEN

ROSELAND

From Harry **to** Charley
Subject: Home
1 August 18:43 GMT

Dear Cuz –

Well, we've moved and you know what? This new house is pretty nice. I've got my own bathroom, which means Charlotte can't flush my toothbrush down the loo 'by accident'. It also means I don't have to share her old bath water – which I didn't like, cos she always wore all that beauty stuff she stole from Mum, which made the water OILY. Plus, this house is ALWAYS warm and I can see the sea from my bedroom window. Dad likes it, too, cos we have the coastal footpath at the end of our garden, which means he can take Dingbat for LOOOOONG WALKKKKKS without ever having to cross a road, or use a lead (which he hates).

And you know who lives like a ten-minute bike ride away? Bulmer. Me, him, Lucas and Bigstock are all starting at the same school next year (cos Bigstock didn't get in to his other school, which I think he's kind of pleased about). Dad said this summer holiday is probably gonna be the best summer holiday ever, cos the Riddles family will finally get to hang out together as a whole FAMILY for the first time in YEARS!

BTW – U don't have to GBTM soon, cos I'm gonna see you next week. Ha!

Harry

World of ZOMBIES
Community Forum

10 September 08.07 GMT

Kid Zombie: Walnut? Is that u?

Goofykinggrommet: Hi Harry!

Kid Zombie: How's Australia?

Goofykinggrommet: OMG, I like it. Good waves. Hot. Sky is always blue. How was Spain?

Kid Zombie: Best summer holiday ever!

 Goofykinggrommet: And the Roseland? U like it down there?

 Kid Zombie: Yeah. Every day I ride my bike to school, so no more long car journeys with Dingbat, who always had really bad wind.

 Goofykinggrommet: COOOL!

 Kid Zombie: And you know I'm MLG now, right?

 Goofykinggrommet: Uh-huh.

Kid Zombie: OK, so I want you to meet a couple of new guys who want to play with us. darkassassin300 meet goofykinggrommet!

Darkassassin300: Hi!

Goofykinggrommet: Hi!

Kid Zombie: And here's a kid I thought we'd never get online. Walnut meet mjgreatestever.

Goofykinggrommet: Who?

Kid Zombie: I think you will probably know him better as Ed Bigstock. Start blasting, Ed!!!

Thank you Loulou and Jessica Alderson for steering me through playground texting protocol on book 3. Thanks also to the Howard family – Kitty, Florence, Lilla, Sarah and Mark. And the Churchill family – Bea, Harry, Arthur, Ricky and Charlotte. Also Lettie, Jonathan and Lucy Neame for explaining how a kid can go from being a single Pringle to a taken bacon.

Thanks also to Andy McNab for being kind enough to contribute some wise words on book 4 and my apologies again for the back cover.

Thanks also to Shaun Parker at PGL for showing me around and then answering all my many emails.

And thanks to Gemma Mayle for Wilson Riddles's most excellent iPad drawings.

And, finally, thank you Nikalas for all your terrific work.